5 Prose Fictions
Lucy R. Lippard

1. The Cries You Hear
2. New York Times IV
3. Headwaters
4. Into Among
5. First Fables of Hysteria

I. The Cries You Hear
Lucy R. Lippard

The rocks trembled every day for over two months and in parts of Tibet a sick person or a woman who had given birth to a child was carefully prevented from sleeping. Sometimes the flower is so constructed that the insect cannot get at the nectar without brushing against a stigma which, perhaps because males tend to fall asleep more rapidly than females after intercourse, returns to stone needles. In the process of collapse the star's outer layers compress. Lying naked in the pouring rain, our wetness the world's wetness, our hard bodies the makings of rock. We took no photographs. The vacant plains were a featureless screen on which we projected our memories of rivers forests oceans and mountains, of elsewhere -- quick! Before it....

Meanwhile the females of the indispensable earthquake rest quietly in the half-closed blossoms, sharing the power of sleep, oblivious to our pain. I was long in doubt concerning the origins of these conditions of stress, horror and exhaustion. That two different organisms should have simultaneously adapted themselves to each other. During the third severe shock the trees were so violently shaken that the birds flew out with frightened cries. Bubblelike cavities formed by expanding gas. Solid pieces blown violently out of the womb. Glass surfaces, brittle and gleaming, formed by rapid solidification. Touch me here. Wrinkles, pores in the earth's skin, basalt lavas swelling from beneath, channeled in fissures, dust and ash. The cries that you hear are only the continuing shock of life.

*

" It is a fatal delusion which presents the earth as the lower half of the universe and the heavens as its upper half. The heavens and earth are not two separate creations, as we have heard repeated thousands and thousands of times. They are only one. The earth is in the heavens. The heavens are infinite space, indefinite expanse, a void without limits; no frontier circumscribes them, they have neither beginning nor end, neither top nor bottom, right nor left; there is an infinity of spaces which succeed each other in every direction."

*

A mountain chain is an effective barrier. The slow movement of underground waters carrying silica into sandstone. Limestone metamorphosed is marble. Bedding planes obscured and mineral impurities drawn out into swirling streaks and bands, swirling streaks and bedding planes obscured. He is tall and arrogant, questioning and vulnerable. Cold tar will shatter if struck but will flow downhill if left undisturbed for a long time. Shattered and flowing, flowing and shattered if struck. Hard things that were soft. Soft things that were hard. Hot things that were cold. Cold things that were hot. Wet things that were dry. Dry things that were wet. Old things that were young. Young things that won't be old. It stops somewhere? Prove it.

Under the mist a solid prose of rocks, rocks and water, hard rocks and flowing water, safe rocks and treacherous water. Rough rocks, motion frozen to the touch, thorny black volcanic piles, a vein, an aggregate, a channel worn away, a pit blown or swirled out, grains, knife edges vertical. And smooth rocks, covered with pale and slippery algae, soothed to a fine old gentleness. Patterns of water, ancient muds, slow curves.

In some alpine mountains high above the timberline, sheets of frost-shattered rock fragments creep slowly down the valleys making curious tounguelike forms. My mouth. My tongue makes love to my mouth, searching its cavities for the softest, wettest places to fondle, sliding past and over the hard sharp teeth so that it hurts a little, overlapping, lapping its own roughness, slipping across the toothmounds under the gums and falling into the dark throat. Craving in. Prose, not poetry. Its tentacles reach in more directions at once, from a solider base, at a natural pace. It circles and radiates, has a core and a skin and a network of capillaries instead of only arteries. Memories wear away the present to an older landscape.

My leg, thicker at the top than at the bottom, stronger at the bottom than at the top, stranger at the top than at the bottom, more useful at the bottom than at the top. At the top, plump flesh held firmly between thumb and foreginger, a few long fine hairs on the broadest whitest part. Smooth and soft and secret lining where other hairs intrude from other sources -- darker, coarser. A crease separating the leg from the rest of the body, a crease that changes character as the leg is used for different things, a soft crease when I am sitting, a mysterious crease when I am lying with one leg curled to my stomach, no crease at all when I am walking, but creased again when running, sometimes. A taut surface when held back, a valley between bulges when not. A leg slimming gradually to a knotted center where the bones assert themselves. A hard hairy hilltop, then a wrinkled old topography flattened into valleys. A leg that swells again, harder this time, smooth again, with a neatly turning strength of its own, a leg that is straight in front and soft-hard in back, flat then rounded, a leg that finally gives way to ankle and foot, the working parts detached from pleasure places above. The bony not so pretty skeletons of motion, fleshed only around the ankle bones, arched over the instep and finally twice in touch with the earth.

*

Each major time unit is brought to a close by orogeny, also called revolution. Disturbance, disruption, disintegration, under pressure. Even the strongest rocks may develop fractures. Deep decay and rotting of igneous and metamorphic rocks, from blocks to egg and sphere shapes. Water entering into union with minerals. Metamorphic rocks have undergone kneading and shaping, baking and shaking, shale turning to slate when split by cleavage, by slippage, during the process. Slate when struck sharply rings metallically. Clay comes in all colors. Playing the geomorphic role of a weak rock, staring at each other but not speaking until finally. A poetic geology to take back to the red hills, white clay to merge as pink. Isolated submarine mountains, the ocean floor pulled apart here, causing a rift, a certain cruelty. Alone is better I say. Then stop the invasion. If you see two scorpions together they are either making love or one of them is being eaten. Aries energy stepped back into the earth. My rock, your mesas. Ice needles pry apart joint blocks, tremendous pressures and bare high cliffs fall off into conical forms, especially in dry climates. Niches, shallow caves, rock arches, pits, cliff dwellings. Come now. Yes/No. In deserts, flash floods and earthflows, mudflows result from the inability of the dry land to permeate the permafrost. Shrinking and swelling. Given sufficient time, barriers can be broken down and new topographies arise. An unbridgeable gulf does not exist between organic and inorganic matter.

II. New York Times IV
Lucy R. Lippard

"Even after years of residence in a big town the Aries subject will feel the call of the wild, will have an innate longing for fresh air, the wide open spaces, the 'feel' of nature....ardent, passionate,quick-tempered, given to volcanic love affairs of short duration....can't stand the meek, secretive and servile....When life becomes dull and placid, you'll be inclined to stir up mischief,quarrel just for the hell of it....."

Looking down into a long oval bathtub at the naked body of a woman stretched full length under green water,feet braced at the far end under old-fashioned ornamental faucets in the shape of spitting heads. Her arms float loosely at her sides, her breasts, nipples erect, lifting bouyantly to the surface, are a different color pink above and below the water. A rectangular piece of amber soap floats to the right by her knee. Below it a dark patch of pubic hair grows up toward the surface like a sea plant; her stomach is distorted by the moving water into a freely contoured oval.

Fucking somebody else hasn't changed my feelings about him, but intensified them. At the same time, it was a direct and instinctive reaction against him, his possessiveness. Even now he isn't so much hurt as in a primitive rage at his own vulnerability, at being lied to. No attempt to understand the love involved in the lie or the restrictions on me that led to it. I know he's been "unfaithful". I don't want to know how or with whom. I don't want to dwell on it because it would give him too much power over me. His lies haven't been told and mine have. So much easier to not lie, to simply <u>cmit</u> betrayals. Why can't I explain these things to him? I'm a writer. I'm supposed to be able to express myself. But I say things I don't mean in the process of trying to say what I do mean well enough. If words weren't "easy" for me I would say less things wrong. He freezes everything I say and won't let me try to say it better. I'm always held to the half-formed and inaccurate. You <u>said</u> ,he's always yelling at me. Yes, I said, but I didn't say it right and so I'm trying again. It's so bleeding hard to say anything right,so anyone else can understand.

Putting myself on paper.

Putting myself down on paper.

Putting myself down.

Keep writing and maybe I won't have to talk. I can feel him lurking back there. Everything physical between us is humiliating. The faces

I make when I cry. The moves toward each other and then the rejections. The faces he makes when he doesn't cry. I wish I knew how to stop it. I wish I knew if I were afraid of our coming apart, or of defeat.
The Waverly Place apartment -- fifth floor, small and prim with a kitchenette hidden by louvred doors always left open, a pink tub and green tiles, a large window in the bedroom. I slept on the couch in the other room because once when I was sleepwalking I almost climbed out of the bedroom window. Shared with two other women. They didn't like my friends, who were bums, but literate. I wasn't as clean as they were, and left soon.
(If I love D as much as I think I do, why am I risking so much by sleeping with O? Sexually there was no need for it.)
The Seventh Street place. Eighteen dollars a month. An outside bathroom shared with a drunken Puerto Rican seaman whose wife was flipping out and wouldn't let him in the apartment during the day. He read the newspaper and drank beer and smoked in the toilet. I had chronic diarrhea and had to bang on the door and plead. I shared my phone with the guy upstairs who had a stove, which I didn't have. The woman who got the seaman's apartment after they left shared my phone too but she didn't have anything I needed. She had an ironing board but I'd given up ironing. Except she read out loud from Joyce better than anyone I've ever heard. My parents didn't like to visit.
(The need, more likely, was to assert myself, to convince myself I was or am independent, relatively free to choose for myself. The first time I saw him needing me more than I needed him I felt trapped.)
Four tiny rooms on 14th street. A little better. We sat in the sink and showered with a rubber hose. When I moved in with him the cabinet under the sink was overflowing with hundreds of filthy socks. Once someone broke in and took only a radio, a can of beer, and a pair of sunglasses.
(I liked and admired O for a long time but wasn't particularly attracted to him physically. When I realized we were going to have an affair, though, I had waves of overwhelming desire at odd times, like sitting next to him in a taxi after a good lunch, or running into him on the street. These were stronger than anything I ever felt in bed with him.)
Avenue C. I always enjoyed showing off how I could fix up these holes in the wall with no money and a coat of paint, furniture from the street. Junkies broke in at least once a week but we had nothing worth taking. I hid the typewriter in the kitchen bathtub under a counter

of dirty dishes. They threw my poppit pearls all over the house in a rage. A poet friend jumped out of the window of the top floor apartment that we'd found for him. I saw him go by.
(O's odd wisdom is particularly sympathetic in someone who so clearly doesn't know how to use it for his own contentment. He answers everything in me D rejects and dislikes. I pity O for his weaknesses but admire the way he fully acknowledges them. It takes a certain courage.)
West 25th Street. A short stay. The Excelsior Hotel. "Transients Welcome."Greasy stove and icebox. Window on an airshaft. D left my typewriter in a cab. The shower was miles away along a pale green corridor lined with salesmen and curious stains.The Broadway Central -- another hotel,much later. I ran away from home. Huge broad corridors patrolled by rats. A room with 15' ceilings and paper curtains covered with obscene roses the size of grapefruit.No bedspreads. Stained sheets. Beautiful old woodwork around the unusable fireplace. Scary elevators. Later several welfare children died in them. Graffiti on the bedroom walls. One floor closed because of a fire a decade ago. A few years later the whole thing fell down.Making love his toenails scratched me.
(Sometimes, more often now, I feel lousy and inadequate for loving D. I've told him I don't know whether I love him or whether he is just a challenge. At the same time, my feelings for him haven't been affected at all by seeing O. Men won't believe it's possible to love two people at once.)
Broome Street loft. We were alone in the building. Something mysterious and Chinese went on three nights a week on the ground floor. No hot water in the living space so I pushed a sink on wheels with a bucket under it for a drain to the back to wash the dishes. Potbelly stove and Jean Shepherd.A Hotel Butter advertisement printed on the bricks agross the street. Great sunsets. Too many flights up. I was getting tired of supporting him and he never read what I wrote.
(These overemotional scenes prove he still wants me? Sometimes I feel him ebbing away from me and I force the tensions simply to make him acknowledge that I exist. I wish there were a pleasanter way of doing it.)
"....few women have knotty fingers,for few women are gifted with the talent of combination.... more tact than science, more quickness of concpetion than strength, more intuition than reasoning. It would be otherwise if they had strongly knotted fingers; then they would yield less easily to the inspirations of fantasy...."
Maps of places I've been and haven't seen yet. Projections at best, and all too close to home.

III. Headwaters

Lucy R. Lippard

<u>For reasons of their own, women are suspicious of diving and frown on their menfolk going down. D-----, who has starred in several underwater films, has never received a fan letter from a woman.</u>
(Jacques Cousteau)

We are already down there. We have already gone down, our breasts bumping the boulders struggling to rise. Our menfolks don't know where to send the fan letters. Can dive, but not delve. Perhaps far down are boundaries between layers of water not obvious at the surface of the sea and quite independent of surface phenomena. Not just still waters. Rapture of the depths. At a town called Headtide there is an old white church unconsciously marking with its spire the spot where the Sheepscott River, short and wide, a tidal estuary, comes to an end in a stony brook and then goes underground. The term tidal wave is loosely applied. Some rivers braid long plaits of sand with thinning streams, and others -- always full, muddy, and sated-- lag in fat banks. Tides are most marked when the sun is nearest the earth. Tides thigh tickling, oozing over the edges and hummocks, a band of foam, making liquid land. Creeps up me towards immersion. Hold your waters. Making waves, seeing red. I flow she flows we flow. Lunar and solar tides coincide, are fully cumulative only twice each lunar month. While fans unfold, snap shut, and leave the flowers no escape. Underwater, irregularities rise and, cursing, fall. Two or more wave patterns at the same place and time. There can, however, be indepdendent waves. And long rivers pass through different landforms like changing lovers. Impatiently cutting gorges, willing waterfalls and rapids to flatness. Unfamiliar bodies hurled at each other. Beneath the rumbling, boulders lurk and lurch, needing a pool.

*

My travelling dreams are washed in foreign waters. In one I swim along a beach. The water is warm and the same pale blue as the sky -- bleached but not burning. Behind me swims a large black dog and before me floats a group of exotic birds, brilliant pink feathers wet but still light, raised above the water in a tangle of wings. The end of the beach is distant; all sand, no rocks or trees in sight. My swimming is leisurely but purposeful. In another dream I wake alone and rush to find my lover. He is in the bathtub and I yell desperately at him: Did I sleep alone last night? Did I sleep alone last night? Another night, my child, my lover and I are going to see a lighthouse through a swamp. The waterway is not very wide. Trees hang dense over the edges but in the center where we swim it's blue, unshaded. A long trip to make boatless, but we are swimming, accompanied at times by a fat friend. I'm not struck by the fact that we are swimming so much as by the length of the trip, not tired so much as a little bored. Once again the water is tepid, body temperature, lulling. The lighthouse when we get there is on a broader bay, still inland, mountains in the distance. There is some talk of leaving and returning in the afternoon. But there isn't time.

*

The waters broke with no warning. Lie still, pretend while it crests. Above our caves the divers' forms pass dimly, unaware. Destructive advances of the sea upon the coasts have two distinct origins: Dreams like sunwarmed flats when the tide comes in very slowly, visibly; earthquakes and storms. Neither related to the tide, and often not actually waves. Floating, I am a fleshly layer between sea and sky. Why go down? Letters melt and corals build. Why go down and not feel the moon in the pit of your stomach? Or hear ripples whisper on the floor? The ocean's bedrock blurred. Unexpected, the cold and purifying northern channels. With no warning, water on the brain the belly breast and buttock. Internal waves stained pink affecting everything (above and below). It doesn't hold water, that's all. Divers make holes in the bubbles and we are already down there, waiting till they stop pouring oil on the waters, stop throwing rocks, sinking ships, turning the tides.

IV. Into Among
Lucy R. Lippard

Stepping down and out. Someone else can move into this house. It looks o.k. from the outside but the inside needs some work. I only regret how long it took to get down those stairs to the basement. Overhead the pretty flowered curtains make wavered patterns on the sunny floor. A tomato is rotting fuzzily in the icebox drawer and other closets capture other odors, other faults. Under the bed dust gathers roses smell acrid. The sheets at the hamper's bottom were stained last winter, not since. I've opened the windows but not the doors. It's all yours, if you want it.

*

Nesting fantasies. I am high in the tallest tree in the world and it sways in the wind. Exhilarating, precarious. I cling to my egg which is disguised as the sea. When the fish hatches I swim through the air until I find a cave, brown, humid, and grainy, where after a night with the boulder another egg is laid, this one transparent. I'm happy watching the beginnings of a new dream. It sometimes has petals, sometimes blades. One morning the walls are opaque and that's that. Dead leaves turn to stone and I would leave but for the field of snakes that writhe beyond the entrance.

*

Shuttered. Unhinged. Falling off the roof. A nice white clapboard house with a soft green lawn, lace curtains at the windows, roses on a trellis over the door, the old fanlight sparkling when the light hits it. We need a very long time to move up the flagstone walk. In the process a war takes place, peace reigns, men land on the moon and women defend it, black blankets of oil are thrown across birds' coffins and the sea stinks. Still the little house remains, the sun always dappling its freshly painted walls, the sound of piano scales twinkling delicately behind the curtain of warmth. When we reach the door we are exhausted, gray, crippled, and in pain. The doorknob, though brilliantly brass, is cold to our touch and the door sticks. It takes our last strength to open it and throw ourselves across the threshold onto what should be a rosy hearth but is instead a deep dark well, the bottom of which, at this telling, we have not reached.

V. First Fables of Hysteria
(rough draft -- Lippard)

Once upon a time there was a little girl, though she was not in fact such a little girl because she was the child of giants, the ones who inhabited this world in the beginning. They had been exiled from the larger land by the Little People, who could move and think so much faster. This girl stood, most of the time, with one foot on a rock in the sea, and one foot on a hill of clay, trying to make up her mind which way to turn. The other children had made up their minds a long time ago, or had had their minds made up for them. The ones playing in the hills had red skin and the ones playing in the sea were blueish white. As time passed, they were slowly sinking to the scale of the place they had chosen. The undecided girl was in danger of becoming both, or neither, and never shrinking.

While she waited, a violent storm came up and lashed at the rock on which she stood with such force that she fell forward into the sea. But the foot on land had by now taken root in the clay and could not be moved, so the little girl lay face down in the sea and her body became a new continent, attached to the old, the red-earthed one, by a natural bridge which led to the bottom of the sea before it climbed to land again. The other giant children were so terrified by her fate that they shrank all at once to the size of humans as we now know them. For eras into the future, no one would inhabit the new continent. Finally it became a refuge for those who did not fit in the other world, a refuge for the dreamers, the failures, the geniuses, and the distraught. Many of these were women and they named their fertile land in honor of the little girl who wanted both worlds -- Hysteria.

*

From the other continent, this place became known as the land of Either-or, for like its child-mother, the inhabitants refused to be confined to a single choice. This was especially important to the women, who tended to be the strongest members of society because of their great determination never to be trapped again in a single role. Because of their reluctance to reject, to confine, their laws were the laws of acceptance and contradiction. Logic was anathema, and when a recent immigrant would venture to use it, s/he was led gently into a gigantic thicket, a maze, and told that it had a logical exit and an illogical exit. No one had ever left through the logical exit because its narrowness frightened the seekers, and the illogical exit, once found, was broad and welcoming.

*

The hystery of this land was, therefore, also a mystery. It flowed and changed according to the tellers' lives, according to the tellers' moods and values, which shifted in turn as society grew and changed. Thus fact <u>was</u> fiction, and there was no separation between them. Hystery did not have to be wrenched out of place to be rewritten. There was no need for religion because myth was reality, and the yearly rites, based on the cyclical changes of nature, reflected the changes that took place in the womb, the hyster, as well as in the imagination. The latter was celebrated each year with The Changing of the Mind, when everyone turned themselves inside out, trying to become what they were not and opening themselves to all possibilities. Greed and ambition rarely had time to take root. The process of yearly rebirth took great courage, and those who became too attached to the status quo were requested to return to the other continent, which was known in Hysteria as the land of the busy dying.

*

.....

5 Prose Fictions
Lucy R. Lippard

New Documents (25)
978-1-953441-08-9

Printed by die Keure
Edition of 500

© 1976 / 2022